Walk On!
a guide for babies of all ages

Marla Frazee

Harcourt, Inc.

Orlando
Austin
New York
San Diego
Toronto
London

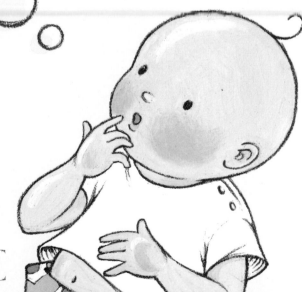

To my son Graham—off to college

F
FRA

www.HarcourtBooks.com

Library of Congress Cataloging-in-Publication Data
Frazee, Marla.
Walk on!: a guide for babies of all ages / by Marla Frazee.
p. cm.
1. Infants—Walking—Juvenile literature. I. Title.
RJ134.F73 2006
612'.044'083—dc22 2004029895
ISBN-13: 978-0152-05573-8
ISBN-10: 0-15-205573-8

H G F E D C B

Manufactured in China

The illustrations in this book were done in black Prismacolor pencil and gouache on Strathmore 2-ply cold press paper, with rubylith. The display and text type were set in PraterSans and PraterScript.
Color separations by Bright Arts Ltd., Hong Kong
Manufactured by South China Printing Company, Ltd., China
This book was printed on totally chlorine-free 100 gsm Munken Print.
Production supervision by Ginger Boyer

Designed by Scott Piehl

Is sitting there on your bottom getting boring?

Has lying around all the time become entirely unacceptable?

It is time to learn how to walk!

The first thing you've got to do is stand on your own two feet.

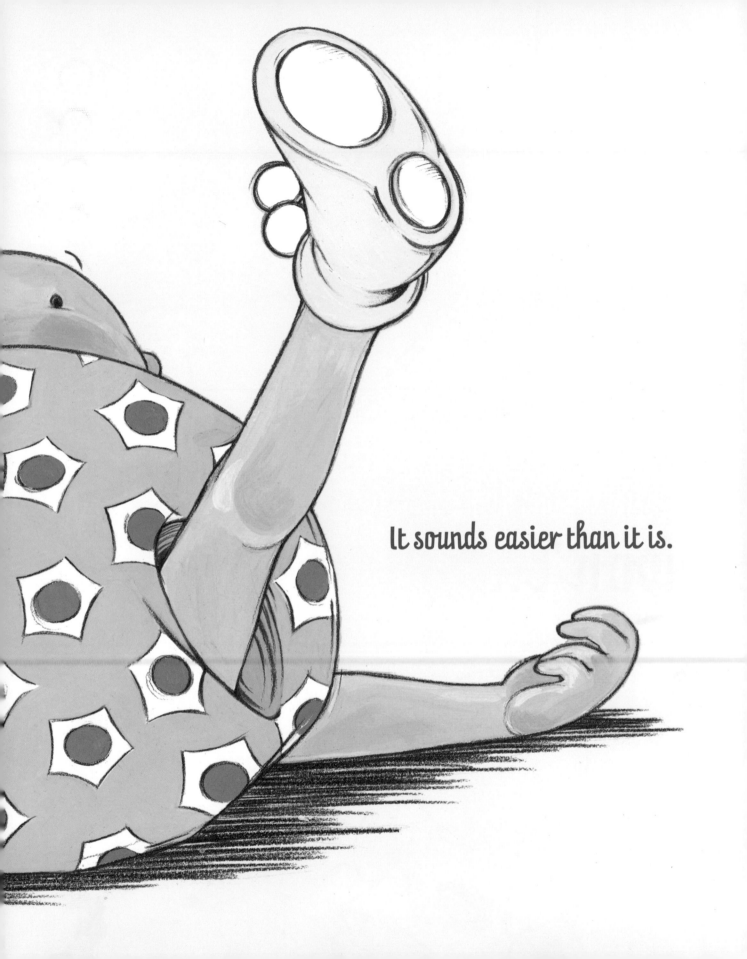

It sounds easier than it is.

You will need support.

This is tricky because sometimes what you think will support you

won't.

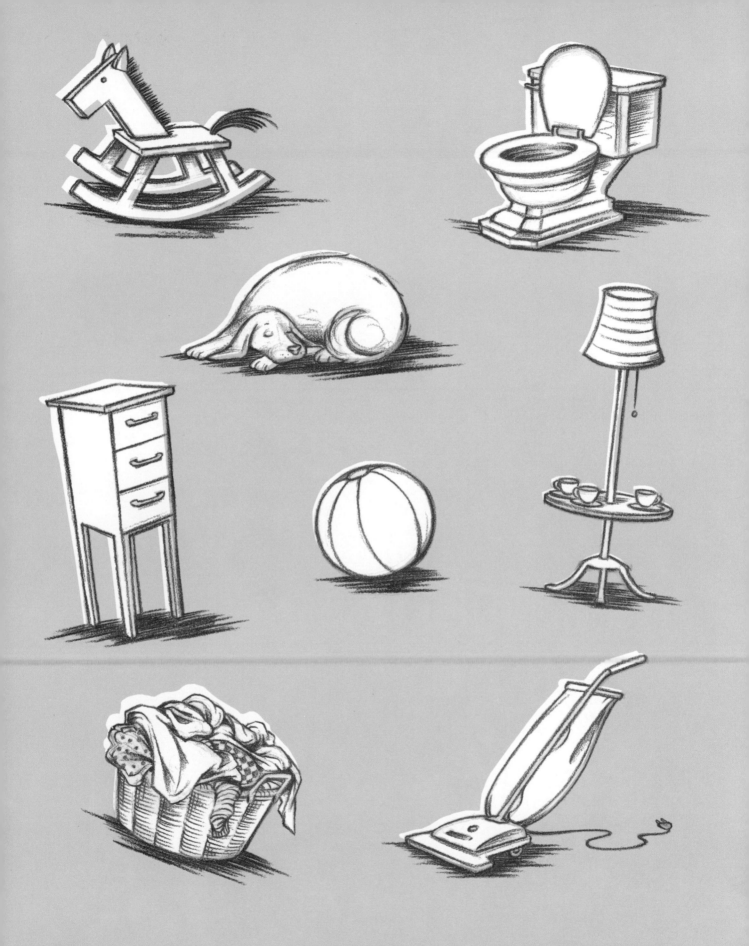

Be careful
of things
that are wobbly.

You don't want
anything to fall
on top of you.

Stay away from
fragile stuff, too.

You don't need
something new
to cry about.

Now. Get a grip.   Pull yourself up.

Stand.

Are your knees buckling?
That's okay.
Straighten up.
See how different
everything looks from here?

Find your balance.

It may take some time.

Remember to
breathe.

Feel the sway,
but don't let it
tip you over.

When you think
you've got it...

let go!

Ooops.

It is very common
to fall down.

Hey, it's okay.

Go ahead and cry
if it helps.

Feel better now?

You can try again, but first,
run down the checklist:

are your **socks** BUNCHING UP?
are your **shoes** TOO TIGHT or TOO LOOSE?
is your **diaper** WEIGHING YOU DOWN?

Fix whatever you can before you start over.

Once you can stand up
without holding on to anything,
get ready to take that first step.

Make sure the path ahead of you is clear. You don't want any obstacles blocking your way or any rough patches tripping you up.

Block out all those voices saying:

Then . . . when the time is right for you . . .

Take the first step.

And another.

And another.

It gets easier, huh?

Baby,
you ar
walkin

Beautiful.